8/13

RSPCA

Animal  Tales

Lost in
Translation

Lost in Translation

Helen Kelly

RANDOM HOUSE AUSTRALIA

A Random House book
Published by Random House Australia Pty Ltd
Level 3, 100 Pacific Highway, North Sydney NSW 2060
www.randomhouse.com.au

First published by Random House Australia in 2012

Addresses for companies within the Random House Group can be
found at www.randomhouse.com.au/offices.

National Library of Australia
Cataloguing-in-Publication Entry

Author: Kelly, Helen
Title: Lost in translation/Helen Kelly
ISBN: 978 1 74275 340 9 (pbk)
Series: Animal tales; 7
Target Audience: For primary school age
Subjects: Animals – Juvenile fiction
Dewey Number: A823.4

Cover photograph © imagestock/Shutterstock
Cover and internal design by Ingrid Kwong
Internal illustrations by Charlotte Whitby
Internal photographs: image of cat by iStockphoto; image of horse
by Lenkadan/Shutterstock; image of tick by ninjaMonkeyStudio/
iStockphoto
Typeset by Midland Typesetters, Australia
Printed in Australia by Griffin Press, an accredited ISO AS/NZS
14001:2004 Environmental Management System printer

Random House Australia uses papers that are natural, renewable
and recyclable products and made from wood grown in sustainable
forests. The logging and manufacturing processes are expected to
conform to the environmental regulations of the country of origin.

Chapter One

Cassie Bannerman flipped over the sign on the deli window from 'closed' to 'open' and unlocked the door. Her dad, Alex, was already getting the coffee machine ready for the morning rush and she took a seat at the counter to finish her breakfast. The gorgeous cheese and bacon muffin was still warm from the oven. Her dad had been up for hours, getting the day's baking done before she had even left for school. She was about to tell him for the millionth time that he really was the best baker in the world, when the door jangled open and Dr Joe Stoppard, the vet from the RSPCA clinic and shelter further up the street, wandered in looking very much in need of coffee.

'Morning, Dr Joe!' said Cassie. Dr Joe was often the first customer of the day and usually stayed for a bit of a chat. Cassie loved animals and one day hoped to become a vet herself, so she was always interested to hear about the comings and goings at the RSPCA.

'Ah, perfect! Just the thing,' said Dr Joe as Alex put down a beautifully brewed cup of coffee on the counter in front of him.

Gladiator, Cassie's beloved tabby cat, swaggered over and gently leapt onto Cassie's lap. After a bit of a wriggle to find the comfiest spot, he purred himself loudly to sleep.

'Gladiator came from our RSPCA shelter, didn't he, Cassie?' asked Dr Joe.

'Yes he did, but way before you first arrived here. He was a tiny kitten then and now he's just about as big as he could be. He must be four years old,' said Cassie, stroking the sleeping cat.

'Well, we're hoping there are lots of other people like you out there who will give a kitten a loving home in the next few weeks,' said Dr Joe as he took his first sip of coffee.

'Yesterday an inspector brought in

a mother cat that had been found on some unused bushland near the tennis courts. She was doing her best to feed a litter of six kittens. They're tiny, even though I think they're about eight weeks old. Both mum and kittens are badly malnourished, but I think a few good meals and lots of TLC will see them come good.'

'Six kittens!' squeaked Cassie.

'Make that eleven kittens . . .' said Dr Joe.

'Eleven?' Cassie was confused.

'Yes. We were just closing up last night when an elderly lady came in with a big box. A mother cat had given birth to five kittens in her garden shed! The mother is microchipped, but we haven't been able to locate her owner yet. The babies are only a few days old; their eyes aren't even open.

They're lucky to be alive, really. It's been pretty cold at night.'

'Goodness, the cattery at the shelter must be overflowing,' mused Cassie.

'Yes, the new holding area was finished just in the nick of time,' said Dr Joe. 'Though it still looks a bit basic. We might need to raise some funds before we can get it properly equipped, but in the meantime it's good to have the extra space.'

'Ha! Wait until they all start growing and running around,' said Cassie. 'It'll be a complete madhouse!'

'They'll be with us for a while too,' added Dr Joe. 'They need to be around twelve weeks old before we can adopt them out, and then only if they're in perfect health,' said Dr Joe.

'Hey, Dr Joe, you could turn part of the new holding area into a kitten playground,' suggested Cassie.

'There'd certainly be plenty of space now and it'd be great that they could be out in the fresh air, all together and yet still safely closed in,' agreed Dr Joe.

'You'd need a lot of new stuff, though,' Cassie pondered aloud. 'Scratching posts and some of those towers, so the kittens could jump from one to the other. And lots of balls and bells and tunnels, of course!'

Alex looked over at Joe and they both shook their heads slightly while they tried not to smile. When Cassie was on a roll, there was really no stopping her.

'And litter! You're going to be needing so much more litter,' she continued.

Dr Joe was finishing up his coffee and was about to leave when Cassie's chatter came to a sudden stop and she jumped to her feet. The forgotten Gladiator was not impressed and grouchily glared at Cassie before sloping off to find a more relaxing place to snooze.

'Dr Joe, you need to raise funds for the kittens right now. I'm going to think of something that will raise enough money to create a playground for them!' Cassie was very excited.

'Now that,' said Dr Joe, 'is a great idea!'

'I just have to think of the perfect thing to do,' Cassie went on. 'Maybe a sponsored walk? Or a raffle? What about a cake sale? Guess the weight of the kitten?'

'Why don't you pop in this afternoon?'

said Dr Joe. He was well aware that it might be some time before Cassie ran out of ideas and he didn't want to be late for work. 'Ben is coming over to have a look at the kittens. Perhaps you can get him interested in your fundraising idea. I'm sure the two of you will come up with something.'

'Sounds perfect. Thanks, Dr Joe. I'd love to see the kittens!' said Cassie.

'Thanks for the coffee, Alex. I'm ready to face the day,' said Dr Joe, getting up and walking towards the door. 'It's going to be a busy one. Not only is the shelter overrun with cats, but within a few minutes it's going to be overrun with students too!'

'Vet students?' asked Alex.

'Yes, four of them. They're all in their first year of university studying Vet Science.

I think I'll have my work cut out for me today!' said Dr Joe as he headed out into the sunshine.

'Bye, Dr Joe,' Cassie yelled after him, her mind still racing with ideas for the fundraiser.

Chapter Two

'So how much are you hoping to raise?' asked Ben.

'Well, I don't know, as much as we can. Anything at all will help. We just need to think of something that will attract people's attention and make them want to give us their money,' said Cassie as the two friends walked home from school. 'My head's been bursting with ideas all day,' she said, 'and I've eventually narrowed it down to my Top Ten Fundraising Ideas!'

With that, Cassie drew a huge piece of paper from her schoolbag and handed it to Ben. It was filled with writing from top to bottom.

'That's way more than ten!' said Ben, appalled that she might actually make him read them all.

'Okay, maybe fifteen. Twenty, tops, but they're all good ideas! I thought we could read through them together and decide which one would be best,' said Cassie.

Ben glanced down the list while Cassie continued to chatter away.

'If we did it at the dog park on a busy

Saturday, there would be a lot of people with pets around. We could make some big, colourful posters and put them up all over the place before then so that everyone would know about it in advance and bring money.'

In spite of himself, Ben was being dragged in. Cassie's enthusiasm was infectious, and as he glanced down Cassie's list of admittedly great ideas, Ben had one of his own.

'So, which one do you like best?' she asked.

'It's not one that's on the list, but I think it could be good. Better than good; it could be huge!' said Ben.

'What is it?' Cassie demanded.

'How about a charity dog-wash?' He

paused uncertainly, and when Cassie didn't say anything he ploughed on. 'We could do it at the dog park and charge ten dollars for each dog. It'd be great fun too, don't you think?' Ben thought it really was a fabulous idea but he'd rarely seen Cassie speechless. Was she annoyed that he hadn't picked one from her list?

Finally she spoke. 'Ben!' she shrieked. 'That is brilliant! It's a perfect idea. Wow, that's fantastic!'

'Okay, Cassie, calm down. You're scaring me now.' Ben grinned. 'We could set up by the gate where there are two water taps,' he continued. 'Have a hose each going in separate directions. We'd need lots of doggy shampoo, but that's all. We wouldn't have to buy anything else.'

'Mum's still got my old baby bathtub in the garage. We could get someone else to join in too and wash the small dogs in the bath,' added Cassie.

'Yeah! Hey I bet we could wash a hundred dogs if we were there all day!'

'Why don't we do it this Saturday?' suggested Ben.

'Sure. That gives us days and days to get everything ready. I could do a poster tonight. Your dad is going to love this!' said Cassie as they reached the clinic and went inside.

Chapter Three

Once inside, Cassie and Ben were surprised to be greeted by a young man in a clean white doctor's coat.

'And what can we do for you today?' he asked. 'Do you have an appointment? Or for that matter, do you have a pet?' he added, looking around them as if to see whether there might be a chance that they were concealing a large dog.

'Oh, um . . .' Ben and Cassie looked at each other as though they might have walked into the wrong place. 'Is Margaret around?' asked Ben.

'I'm over here, Ben! Hi Cassie!' Margaret shouted over from the reception desk. 'This is Peter, one of our work-experience students. It's okay, Peter, this is Dr Joe's son, Ben, and his friend Cassie.'

From behind the stacks and stacks of files piled up on the reception desk popped up one, and then two heads. Within seconds two more students wearing pristine white coats appeared from behind the counter.

'Hello, Ben and Cassie, I'm Grace,'

said a smart-looking girl with beautiful long dark hair.

'I'm Michael,' said a tanned boy with an athletic build. 'It's very nice to meet you both.'

Ben and Cassie didn't know what to say. The vet students were so confident and . . . tall!

'Ah, have you enjoyed your first day?' Cassie managed to ask before the door opened behind them and the fourth white-coated student appeared.

'Oh, another one,' said Cassie with an uncertain smile.

Now Cassie and Ben were completely surrounded by the students.

'Hello,' said the newcomer, and she hurried past them.

'And that's Lauren,' said Peter.

Lauren glanced back with a little smile and then carried on towards Margaret.

'Did you get to watch Dad in action?' asked Ben.

'Yes!' Grace, Michael and Peter said all together.

'It was fascinating! We watched two different dogs undergo surgery,' started Grace.

'Yes, one had been knocked down by a car and had broken his leg badly, but your dad was great!' continued Michael.

'He'll be right as rain in a few weeks!' said Peter.

'And the other had swallowed a piece of Lego,' said Grace.

'And your dad had to put the little

camera down his throat to see just how far it had gone before deciding the best way to remove it.'

'He's fantastic!'

'And the cat. Don't forget the cat.'

'He needed six stitches across his head after getting into a fight with a wire fence.'

'Poor thing.'

'And now we're having a look at some of your dad's old cases.'

Cassie and Ben were losing track of who was saying what. The students were so enthusiastic and all spoke at once. Just then the consulting room door opened and his dad came towards them.

The three students moved as a unit; they just seemed to gravitate towards Dr Joe, and the children were forgotten.

'Did you need us, Dr Joe? Is there something you'd like us to do?' they all asked.

Dr Joe was looking a bit frazzled and Ben understood why. These students were really something else!

Chapter Four

'I think a bit of fresh air is in order,' declared Dr Joe a little desperately.

He had four dog leashes in one hand and four dog singlets in the other. Each singlet was bright blue and had the words 'I'm looking for a home. Interested in adopting a dog? Speak to my walker!' emblazoned across the back.

'Take one of these each,' he said, handing them out. 'Where's Lauren?' he asked, looking around.

'I'm here, Dr Joe. Sorry I was just finishing off –' she began as she came towards them.

'It's okay,' said Dr Joe, cutting her off. 'Just follow me.' He turned on his heel and strode towards the dog-holding area, the students fluttering along behind him.

Cassie and Ben looked at each other and shrugged before following them out.

'This is Bill,' said Dr Joe, introducing a large, cheery-looking, middle-aged man. 'Bill's one of our favourite volunteers and one of our most experienced dog walkers. He's been coming in two evenings a week for over ten years and there is nothing that he doesn't know about dogs! Today, you're all going to help him,' said Dr Joe to the students. 'You met all the dogs earlier, and now Bill has selected a dog for each of you to take for a walk.

'He'll show you where our local park is. There's a fantastic leash-free area in the middle that's fenced in and huge. It's perfect for a really good run. The dogs will wear the singlets, and you'll find that a fair few people will stop to chat about the adoption program and ask for info. Okay, everyone?'

The students were ready for action. As though Dr Joe had fired a starting pistol, they flew towards the dogs like a busy swarm of bees.

Within minutes the dogs and students were lined up and ready to go. Bill was like a Sergeant Major. They walked out two by two. Peter and Bill led the pack with twin German shepherds called Morris and Maud firmly at heel. Then came Michael and Grace; Michael with Muddle, an energetic young kelpie, and Grace with a whippet called Bones, who was almost as elegant as herself. Lauren trailed behind the others with a timid, doe-eyed little bitser called Colin.

'I'll keep them out for an hour; they'll come back exhausted,' said Bill with a wink, leaving Dr Joe to wonder whether he meant the dogs or the students.

Dr Joe turned to Cassie and Ben with a sigh of relief.

'Oh yes, the kittens!' he said. And he turned on his heel once more.

DOG

The cattery was quiet and subdued compared to the rest of the shelter and Dr Joe seemed altogether calmer and more subdued himself.

He pointed to a large cage that had a sack covering the front of it to create a nice dark space inside.

'The kittens are in here,' he said and pulled the cloth cover open halfway. Cassie and Ben peered in and saw five tiny kittens all huddled together beside mum, fast asleep.

'Any luck with the microchip, Dr Joe?' whispered Cassie.

'No, nothing yet,' he replied. 'There's no response from the phone number that's on record. But it's early days. I'm sure someone is missing her; she's been well taken care of. What we do know is that her name is Peppermint.'

'Aww, that's so sweet,' cooed Cassie.

Ben laughed. 'Yeah, good one, Cassie, sweet! Peppermint? Sweet? Get it?'

'So lame,' said Cassie and tried to ignore him.

'Apart from keeping mum well fed, there's really not much we need to do for them right now,' said Dr Joe. 'Just provide a warm, comfortable and quiet environment until they're a bit bigger. They're all in good health, which is lucky,'

Cassie took one last look at the kittens before replacing the cloth and following Dr Joe and Ben into the next room.

'The second lot are in the exercise pen with mum. You can watch them play and then we'll round them up for bed,' said Dr Joe.

'I love your idea about the kitty playground, Cassie,' said Dr Joe, as they watched the tiny kittens crawling and tumbling over each other. 'They really would benefit from the fresh air and just being in a bigger space. Did you think any more about the fundraiser?'

'Of course! It's all decided and the date is set!' said Cassie.

Chapter Five

Later that same evening Cassie was sitting in her favourite homework spot, the table closest to the counter in the deli. The table was scattered with every colour of texta you could imagine and several large sheets of discarded paper.

'Okay, this is the one, Mum. What do

you think?' she said as she held her finished masterpiece up for inspection.

'Wow, it looks very professional! Those colours are really going to stand out. And you've got all the information you need,' said Sam as she read down the page.

Charity dog wash!
This Saturday at the Abbotts Hill Dog Park.
9am-4pm
$10 per dog.
Raising money to help kittens in need at the RSPCA.
See you there.
Don't forget your dog!

'That's great, Cass! It covers everything and your pictures are gorgeous. It's definitely an eye-catcher,' said Sam. 'I might send one to the fundraising people at the RSPCA. I called them today to let them know what you've got planned. They thought it was a great idea and wished you the best of luck.'

'Thanks, Mum. I can't wait until Saturday!' said Cassie.

At that moment, just as Sam was thinking she could probably shut up shop for the night, the deli door opened and a whole group of customers came chattering up to the counter and ordered coffees, hot chocolates and muffins before plonking themselves down at the table across from Cassie's.

Cassie started to clear away her things when she realised that the chattering had stopped and the entire group of new arrivals was looking her way!

'Cassie!' said one of them. 'We met you earlier at the clinic!'

'Oh, hello,' said Cassie, recognising Dr Joe's work-experience students. 'You look different without your white coats on. Have you just finished?'

'Yes,' said Grace, 'we've had such a great day. But what's this you're doing? School project?'

'No, it's just a fundraising thing that Ben and I are doing on Saturday. We're going to try to wash as many dogs as we can to raise money for Dr Joe to spend on the new kittens,' said Cassie as the students passed her poster around so they could all read it.

It was agreed loudly and enthusiastically that the whole idea was wonderful! By the time the students had all read to the bottom of the page, Cassie had enlisted three willing helpers for Saturday and the whole thing looked as though it was going to be as huge as Ben had predicted.

When the students discovered that Cassie wanted to be a vet when she grew up, they spent the next half hour passing on tips and funny stories about their learning experiences.

Cassie was a bit overwhelmed by all the attention. As she looked down the table she realised for the first time that Lauren was there too. The student was slowly sipping tea and seemed happy to let the conversation drift along without her. Cassie wondered if Lauren wasn't as overwhelmed by the other students as she was.

'Well, we better get going!' said Peter,

and the students all stood up. 'Another busy day at the surgery tomorrow, doctors,' he joked. The group left the deli, sounding like a noisy gaggle of geese.

'Switch that sign to closed, would you, Cass?' yelled Sam. 'Let's get this lot sorted out and we'll go and have some dinner,' she said as she came round the counter to clear the table.

She jumped as she saw Lauren and then laughed at herself. 'Oh, sorry, you gave me a bit of a surprise! I thought you'd all left together. Can I get you something else?'

'No, no, sorry,' said Lauren, who was the picture of embarrassment. 'I didn't realise you were closing. I'd better move.'

'Ha!' laughed Cassie. 'Do it carefully or you'll get the Death Stare.'

'Mmm . . .' said Lauren, smiling for the first time. 'I'm quite familiar with the Death Stare.'

Sam stared at them as though they'd both gone mad until she spotted Gladiator. Though the cat appeared very comfortable on Lauren's lap, he had one eye open looking around suspiciously. Sam laughed. 'He's big, but he wouldn't hurt a flea.' She grabbed Gladiator and headed towards his cat bowl. 'Dinnertime for the furry member of the household.'

Chapter Six

By the time Sam came back with three frothy mugs of hot chocolate, Cassie and Lauren were chatting away like old friends.

'It's so different to being at university,' Lauren was saying. 'Today was the first time I'd seen an actual operation. Of course we've all done the theory, but when it came to the real thing, Dr Joe was firing off questions like *'How would you restrain that cat?'* and *'What size needle would I use for this?'* and I just stood there all tongue-tied. I don't think I managed to answer a single question. All the others were jumping up and down to volunteer and shouting out answers to every question almost before it was asked. I don't think I made a very good first impression.'

Cassie and her mum were still grinning at Lauren's very accurate impersonation of Dr Joe and Lauren found herself smiling too.

'I'm sure tomorrow will be better,' said Sam.

'Everyone's different,' said Cassie, 'and Dr Joe knows that. I think by the end of the week he might be wishing he had more students like you.'

'Pick one thing that you loved about today,' said Sam. It was a game she played with her daughter when she'd had a bad day and it always made Cassie feel better.

'That's easy,' said Lauren, still smiling. 'Colin!'

'Ah yes, he's so gorgeous, isn't he?' said Cassie dreamily. 'Those big brown eyes . . .'

Her mother looked at her with a curious expression on her face. 'Who's Colin?' she asked, imagining an attractive young man.

'Colin the dog!' said Cassie.

Sam looked so relieved that Cassie and Lauren fell about laughing.

'I better go,' said Lauren, 'but thank you, both. You've really cheered me up. You're right, tomorrow will definitely be better. And I love your poster, Cassie! Where are you going to put it?'

'I hadn't really thought about it yet,' said Cassie. 'Mum's going to make copies. I guess at all the local shops, at school and at the park, of course.'

'How about I give you a hand putting them up tomorrow?' offered Lauren.

'That would be great, Lauren, thanks! I'll meet you at the clinic after school.'

Chapter Seven

By the time school finished the next day, Cassie had already put up six posters around the buildings. Everybody at school was already talking about it. Cassie's teacher, Miss Smith, had already said she'd be first in the queue on Saturday with her little Jack Russell, Rollo.

Cassie and Ben had just gone home long enough to drop off their schoolbags and pick up Ripper and Florence and then headed straight to the clinic. It was calmer today, and Margaret was clearly visible in her usual spot behind the reception desk.

'Hi Margaret, can we put one of our posters up in here?' asked Ben.

'Of course! In fact, Lauren told me all about it and rearranged the whole noticeboard to make room. See that big space in the middle? That's for you. And maybe put one in the window too, so that everyone can see it from outside,' said Margaret.

'Lauren has just popped out the back with Bill to walk one of the dogs, and I think Grace is keen to help! Dr Joe was so pleased that they're getting involved,' she continued.

Cassie busied herself with posters and tape. As was she standing back to admire her work, Lauren and Grace appeared; Lauren, again with Colin, and Grace, with an old black labrador called Penny. Both dogs looked very attractive in their bright blue singlets.

'Perfect timing!' said Cassie. 'Let's get down to work.'

By the time they unleashed the dogs at the park an hour later, every shop between the clinic and the park had a poster hanging proudly in the window. There was one on every fence post, gate and noticeboard within the park, and they already seemed to be attracting a lot of attention.

Ripper, as usual, led the way, running for the sheer pleasure of it, with Florence hard on his heels, bumbling along cheerfully. Penny seemed happy to stick close to Grace, enjoying the fresh air and the good company, while Colin, growing in confidence, had found a playful border collie puppy, who was quite happy to share his ball.

As they walked they chatted with whoever came their way. Everyone was talking about the charity dog-wash. It had created quite a buzz, and Cassie and Ben's excitement was growing with it; they could talk about nothing else!

'I think Penny's had enough,' said Grace as they were passing their gate for the fifth time. 'We might call it a day.'

'Yes, it's probably time for us to go too. Come on, Ripper!' called Cassie.

Ripper came bounding over and sat obediently while Cassie attached his lead. Florence came too, and Ben was convinced for a split second that she would follow Ripper's good example and let him put her lead on without the usual performance. She sat still until Ben got within an arm's length. Then she set off at a gallop into the centre of the park with Ben at her heels. She loved this game!

As Lauren, Grace and Cassie stood back to enjoy the show, they noticed an elderly woman nearby who they hadn't seen before. She had a Maltese terrier sitting beside her and it looked as though she was trying to coax the dog to its feet. But the terrier seemed quite distressed, and every time it tried to stand it looked really shaky and lay down again.

'Hey, is everything okay?' asked Cassie.

The lady was beginning to get very upset and answered Cassie in quick-fire Chinese. The only words that Cassie could understand were 'Bella, Bella,' but it was obvious that the lady was both very worried and that she spoke no English. Cassie was stumped, but it was clear that the dog was seriously hurt or ill. What could she do?

'Cassie, could you look after Colin for a moment?' asked Lauren, handing Colin's lead over to Cassie. Then she turned to the lady and started talking quickly and confidently to her in Cantonese.

The lady became calmer and more reassured now that she had found somebody with whom she could communicate. Lauren stepped forward and quickly examined the terrier where it lay on the ground before picking it up and cradling it to her chest.

'Let's get this dog to the clinic,' said Lauren.

She turned to the lady and, putting an arm round her shoulder, ushered her out of the park, talking calmly to her the whole time.

Chapter Eight

As they came through the door of the clinic, the other students sensed that something was wrong and crowded around asking questions, questions, questions!

Lauren pushed through and ignored them all, concentrating on the ill dog in her arms.

'Margaret, this is an emergency. We'll need Dr Joe as soon as possible,' she said firmly and continued through to the consulting room with Bella the Maltese and her owner.

The students stepped back at once to give her more space and couldn't help raising their eyebrows at her determined tone.

By the time Lauren laid Bella on the examining table, Dr Joe was there by her side.

'What's wrong?' he asked the owner, but she just stared blankly at him and shrugged her shoulders before looking back at Lauren. Lauren reassured her calmly in Cantonese that everything was okay. Dr Joe raised his eyebrows and smiled at Lauren, suitably impressed.

'This is Cynthia,' said Lauren. 'She's on holiday from China and is staying with her niece in Abbotts Hill. Bella is her niece's dog. They've already been down to the beach for a walk this morning, but it was only this afternoon at the dog park when she noticed that Bella was behaving strangely. She said she seemed disorientated and wobbly on her feet and her bark sounded different.'

All the time she was talking, with an encouraging nod from Dr Joe, Lauren was firmly feeling the dog all over. She had started right at the tip of her nose and spent a long time working her way back down Bella's face to her furry ears. She didn't miss a bit! Dr Joe, with his many years of experience, had already picked up on

Lauren's concerns and had started his search from the back, the very tip of Bella's tail, and was working his way forward.

'So you're thinking –' started Dr Joe as his hands continued searching.

'I'm thinking it must be a tick,' finished off Lauren. 'And judging by the severity of the symptoms, I think it's probably *Ixodes Holocyclus*, commonly known as the paralysis tick. Bella may have picked it up at the beach this morning.'

'I think you're right, Lauren. Pretty spot-on diagnosis,' said Dr Joe. 'Now, all we have to do is find that tick, pronto!'

Chapter Nine

It seemed like a long time later that Lauren gave a triumphant 'Aha!' and smiled at last.

Lauren and Dr Joe had searched the dog three times over and had just begun to consider the possibility that they may need to clip all her hair off to get a better look when suddenly, on the fourth look, Lauren found the horrible little tick stuck right in between two of Bella's tiny toes. It was no bigger than an apple pip!

Cynthia clapped her hands and smiled. No translation was needed to see the relief she felt.

Dr Joe carefully removed the tick with tweezers, popping it into a jar with a lid so that the other students could see it too. It was a useful thing to be able to identify, after all. The students and Cassie and Ben gathered at the door and breathed a collective sigh of relief, but Dr Joe and Lauren both appeared grave.

'It could be another day or two before there's any real improvement in Bella's condition, couldn't it, Dr Joe?' asked Lauren quietly.

'Yes,' replied Dr Joe. 'Bella is not out of the woods yet. Her symptoms could continue to get worse for another forty-eight hours before we see any improvement at all. The most important thing we can do now is keep her still and quiet.

'I'm going to give her this,' he said, filling a syringe. 'It's a mild sedative that will calm her down so that we can set up a drip for the anti-toxin. Then we'll find a quiet spot where we can keep a close eye on her. Will you bring Cynthia up to date? Let her know that she's welcome to visit, but it's unlikely Bella will be fit to go home for a few days yet.'

Lauren sat talking the whole thing over with Cynthia until her niece, Emily, arrived to take her home.

'Thank you so much,' said Emily. 'My poor aunt must have been very distressed. She can't believe her good fortune to have found someone in the dog park who could speak such perfect Cantonese!'

'My grandmother would be happy to hear you say that,' said Lauren modestly. 'My mum moved to Australia when she was just a little girl and completely forgot her Cantonese. So when I was born, my grandmother moved in with us to help look after me and she was determined that I should know my mother tongue. Granny is the only person I ever speak to in Cantonese, but it certainly came in handy today.'

'Handy for us, for sure!' said Emily.

Lauren was the hero of the hour. Once Emily and Cynthia had gone home, all the students wanted to know what had happened in the park and the consulting room. The tick was passed round in its little glass jar, and everyone marvelled at the tiny size of it compared to the huge problems it could cause.

Lauren was a bit embarrassed to find herself the centre of attention but pleased too when Dr Joe started enthusing about her calm and professional attitude, not to mention her hidden talents.

Chapter Ten

Saturday morning arrived at last and with it all the bustle of the fundraiser. Ben and Cassie had been at the park since eight o'clock, getting everything just right. They'd rustled up an old market gazebo from a neighbour and had managed to put it up so that they would be out of the hot sun while they washed. Two long hoses went left and right, away from the taps, and a bright yellow baby bath sat in between them. Dr Joe had donated two large bottles of doggy shampoo, and Ben and Cassie were not going home while there was even a drop left!

Around the gazebo and along the fence in either direction were strings of colourful bunting that had been left over from the Girl Guides cake sale and kindly donated by way of Sarah at school. Several school friends had also made cardboard posters, which were now hung along the fence at regular intervals. Ben and Cassie were feeling pretty proud of themselves. They really hadn't forgotten a thing!

By nine o'clock the dog park was filling up and there was Miss Smith, true to her word, rushing along, dragging a reluctant Jack Russell behind her.

'Morning, Cassie! Morning, Ben! This looks wonderful! Now, Rollo, be a good boy. Here you go, Ben,' she said, handing over Rollo's lead to Ben and a ten-dollar note to Cassie. 'The first of many, I'm sure,' she said.

The vet students turned up next with Bill, as well as two other shelter volunteers, each with a shelter dog in tow and a whole bunch of leaflets to hand out regarding both the cat and dog adoption programmes run by the shelter.

Lauren was to be the money collector for the day and Cassie proudly popped Mrs Smith's ten dollars into the tin.

With all the kerfuffle surrounding the

new arrivals, it was unclear how Ben came to be quite so wet and quite so red in the face while washing little Rollo, but gosh, that dog was shiny and clean at the end of it all.

Cassie, with a dog trainer's insight, had filled her pockets with little liver treats and surprisingly found that the dogs she washed were all pretty well behaved.

It seemed that every dog they knew came through the park that morning and plenty that neither of them had ever seen before: Maguire the ball-obsessed cattle dog, Levi the chihuahua – who was so tiny they only charged five dollars – was the first to experience the luxury of the bathtub, Spinner the Spaniel, Tommy and Tallulah the Aussie Terriers, Barney, Chewy, Dixie, Rex, Rosie, Cookie, Coco, Josie, Cara,

Pumpkin, Pixie, Molly, Yogi . . . The queue went on and on and on.

'Hey, Cassie, it looks like it's going really well,' said Ben's mum, Veronica. 'I've been in line for ages!'

'Oh, hi, Veronica, I didn't see you there. Are you ready for a bath, Florence?' asked Cassie, turning towards the big fluffy Old English sheepdog.

Ben looked up from washing a beautiful little staffy-cross called Milo and sat back on his heels. Florence HATED bath-time and he just had to see how badly this was going to go.

But Ben was a little disappointed. Florence sat still while Cassie soaked her all over with the hose. Florence looked utterly miserable once she was wet but stood calmly while Cassie rubbed on the shampoo and lathered her all over.

The suspense was killing Ben; he was expecting Florence to run for it at any minute. He could feel laughter bubbling up inside him as he dried off Milo and popped the money in the tin.

Cassie carefully rinsed Florence and finished off by giving her the liver treat. Ben was gutted and even Veronica was amazed.

Then, suddenly, as Veronica was thanking Cassie and handing over her money, Florence ran. The lead was yanked from Veronica's hand and Florence headed straight for the gate. Ben ran after her, pleased at least to be proved right about his own dog.

After the whole morning of washing, the grass was wet and a huge, muddy puddle had formed between the dog-wash area and the gate. Florence had clearly spotted it earlier because she headed straight for it and performed a perfect dive right into the puddle's centre. Mud shot out in every direction and Ben was coated in it from head to toe.

Florence's gorgeously clean, silver-and-white coat turned brown and slimy and she sighed in sheer contentment as she did the cockroach – wriggling on her back, legs in the air and clearly loving every minute of it.

By lunchtime the queue was dwindling and when Alex Bannerman turned up at the park with a big brown paper bag, Ben and Cassie realised they were starving. Lauren and Grace were only too happy to take over for half an hour while Ben and Cassie enjoyed the luxury of sitting down and feasting on toasted cheese and tomato sandwiches and the banana and chocolate smoothies that Alex had brought with him.

'I have dessert too!' said Alex as he rushed off back to the deli, only to return minutes later with a huge tray of perfectly iced cookies. All the cookies were in the shape of dogs and cats. 'You can have one each only,' he warned. 'And I will give some to the students and volunteers. Everyone else will have to pay a dollar! It is for a good cause, after all,' he said with a wink to Ben and Cassie.

As Ben and Cassie nibbled away happily, Alex sauntered up to the front of the queue to give Lauren and Grace a cookie for later. He had the tray raised high above his head, balanced perfectly on one hand as though he was in a fancy restaurant. Just as Alex reached the girls, Lauren finished washing Belvedere, a very highly strung giant poodle.

Cassie could see what was going to happen just seconds before it actually did. She jumped to her feet and yelled 'Dad!' but it was as though everything became slow-motion.

Belvedere leapt to his feet and his owner grabbed for his collar just as Alex came between the two of them with his tray held high.

The perfect pirouette that Alex performed won admiring glances from the queue of pet owners. Alex was desperate to save the tray of cookies but, ultimately, there was nowhere else to go – the yellow bathtub full of dog hair and cold soapy water welcomed Alex, bottom-first.

Cassie put her hands over her eyes and only removed them when seconds later a cheer went up from the queue, followed by loud applause. Her dad was sitting almost upright in the baby bathtub. He looked as if he might need a hand to get out . . . but the tray of cookies remained high above his head. Not one had dropped to the floor!

Chapter Eleven

It was at the end of an exhausting day, as Lauren and Cassie were taking down the bunting and Ben was dismantling the gazebo, that Cynthia and Emily walked past.

'Hello Lauren,' said Emily. 'Dr Joe said you would be here. We've just been to pick up Bella. She's made such an excellent recovery and it's all thanks to you!' Emily opened the pet carrier she was carrying to show them the sleepy-looking but healthy Bella inside.

'I don't think she's quite well enough to take a bath here yet. But the next time you have a dog-wash, we'll be first in line,' Emily said as she put enough money into Lauren's tin to pay for several baths.

Dr Joe was the next and last visitor. He ushered the students back to the clinic with the shelter dogs and the tired volunteers, with strict instructions to meet at the deli in twenty minutes.

The day had been an amazing success. Ben, Cassie and Lauren were counting the money as the other students entered the deli. Colin was curled lazily at Lauren's feet with no blue singlet to be seen! And Alex came round the counter and managed to put down a whole tray of milkshakes without any dance moves whatsoever.

Dr Joe stood up and looked down at the group of people stretched across the three tables that had been pushed together. All the students were there, as well as the volunteers and Ben and Cassie, Cassie's parents and his own wife, Veronica. He was so proud of everyone that he could hardly speak.

'Cassie,' he said, 'would you like to tell us how much money you and Ben have raised today?'

Cassie got to her feet, 'Drum roll, please,' she said.

Ben obliged, with his hands on the table top. 'The total is . . . one thousand and forty-two dollars!'

A cheer went up around the table.

'A wonderful achievement, you two,' he said to Ben and Cassie. 'But you know what is an even bigger achievement? You've raised awareness in Abbotts Hill about the plight of abandoned dogs, cats and, particularly, kittens.

'Today we received pledges from people in our own community to adopt every one of the new kittens when the time comes, as well as one of the mummy cats too. I know it's a relief to us all to know that they're going to wonderful homes where they will be loved.

'On top of that, we've had a lot of

interest in our shelter dogs. My wonderful students and volunteers have been out with the dogs every day this week and the knock-on effect is that we have re-homed seven of our long-term residents, as well as one recent arrival, who I know is going to be very happy to be going home with a new owner this evening.'

Lauren blushed before saying, 'Mum and Dad popped into the shelter today to see Colin, who I've been talking about all week. They fell in love with him too, and it just feels great to be able to offer him a new home. I think he'll love living with us.'

Colin would no doubt have agreed completely if he hadn't been snoring contentedly at her feet. It had been a busy day, after all.

'I've had such a wonderful week, Dr Joe,' continued Lauren. 'We've learnt so much.' The other students nodded in agreement. 'Thank you on behalf of all of us.'

'Thanks, Lauren, and to all of you. I wish you well in your careers. I know you'll all make terrific, caring vets in the future,' said Dr Joe. 'I've kept my favourite bit of news for the end,' he continued. 'And I know you'll like this, Cassie. Microchips work! Our lovely little mummy Peppermint has found her way home!

'Her owner contacted us today. Peppermint went missing from home after her family moved house nearly six months ago. They presumed she must have been run over by a car and had just about given up on ever finding her.

'They're going to pick her up in seven weeks, once her kittens are old enough to go to their new homes.

'They've agreed to have her de-sexed too so that there's no chance of the same thing happening again. It's such a good result all round! Well done, everyone!'

A yawning Cassie turned to an exhausted and dirt-covered Ben. 'Want to do it all again next weekend?'

Ben gave a small Florence-like whine as he rested his forehead on the table in front of him.

Cassie patted him on the back. 'What about the weekend after?'

ABOUT THE RSPCA

The RSPCA is the country's best known and most respected animal welfare organisation. The first RSPCA in Australia was formed in Victoria in 1871, and the organisation is now represented by RSPCAs in every state and territory.

The RSPCA's mission is to prevent cruelty to animals by actively promoting their care and protection. It is a not-for-profit charity that is firmly based in the Australian community, relying upon the support of individuals, businesses and organisations to survive and continue its vital work.

Every year, RSPCA shelters throughout Australia accept over 150,000 sick, injured or abandoned animals from the community. The RSPCA believes that every animal is entitled to the Five Freedoms:

Fact File

- freedom from hunger and thirst (ready access to fresh water and a healthy, balanced diet)
- freedom from discomfort, including accommodation in an appropriate environment that has shelter and a comfortable resting area
- freedom from pain, injury or disease through prevention or rapid diagnosis and providing veterinary treatment when required

- freedom to express normal behaviour, including sufficient space, proper facilities and company of the animal's own kind and
- freedom from fear and distress through conditions and treatment that avoid suffering.

TICK PARALYSIS PREVENTION FOR YOUR PET

Paralysis ticks (*Ixodes holocyclus*) are among the most dangerous parasites that can affect your pet.

The paralysis tick is found on the eastern seaboard of Australia, from North Queensland to Northern Victoria, particularly in bushland.

Fact File

How does the tick cause paralysis?

The tick sucks blood from the host animal and secretes saliva that contains toxins. These toxins enter the bloodstream and cause poisoning.

How to identify the paralysis tick

They tend to be light blue to grey in colour, ranging in size from two or three millimetres to as large as 10 millimetres. But even the smallest tick can cause paralysis. Once on the animal, the tick embeds itself firmly into the skin. When an adult tick feeds on blood, it increases in size dramatically.

Symptoms of tick paralysis

- Loss of coordination in the hind legs
- Change in voice or bark
- Retching, coughing or vomiting
- Loss of appetite
- Progressive paralysis to include the forelegs
- Difficulty breathing or rapid breathing

Fact File

What to do if your pet shows symptoms of tick paralysis

1. Keep your pet calm and in a cool, dark place until you take it to the vet.
2. Do not offer food or water, as this may lead to pneumonia and breathing difficulties if your pet can't swallow properly.
3. Seek veterinary attention as soon as possible.

How to protect your pet from paralysis ticks

During the tick season, don't take your dog walking in bushy areas. Keep lawns and shrubs short and remove compost material from backyards.

Search pets every day for ticks: Use the fingertips to feel through the animal's coat. Ticks or tick craters can be felt as lumps on the skin surface.

Although most ticks are found around the head and neck of the animal as well as

Fact File

inside the ears, they can end up anywhere on the body. It is especially important to search long-haired dogs very thoroughly between the eyes and the end of the nose. The most reliable way to locate the ticks is to systematically run your fingers through your cat or dog's coat.

Once located, a tick hook is useful to help remove the tick. If the head is left in, the tick will die anyway and will no longer inject poison. Always assume there is more than one tick and continue your search.

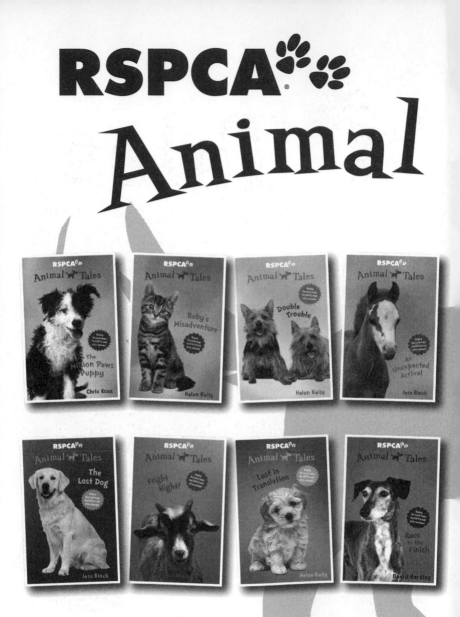

Tales

RSPCA Animal Tales

A New Home for Cocoa

Buying this book helps the RSPCA look after animals!

Helen Kelly

RSPCA Animal Tales

Florence Takes the Lead

Buying this book helps the RSPCA look after animals!

COLLECT THEM ALL

COMING DECEMBER 2012

THERE'S SO MUCH MORE AT RANDOMHOUSE.COM.AU/KIDS